Walter

May the bird of time nest in
your heart

The Bird of Time

The Bird of Time

by
Jane Yolen

Illustrated by
Mercer Mayer

THOMAS Y. CROWELL COMPANY • NEW YORK

Manufactured in the United States of America
L. C. Card 72-139102
ISBN 0-690-14425-3
0-690-14426-1 (LB)

1   2   3   4   5   6   7   8   9   10

In memory of my mother,

Isabelle B. Yolen

Once there was a miller who was named Honest Hans because he never lied or gave false weight. He had an only son called Pieter, whom many considered a fool.

Pieter often sat long hours looking steadily at the sky or a bird or a flower, saying nothing and smiling softly to himself. At such times he would not answer a question, even if someone asked him the time of day or the price of a sack of flour.

Yes, many considered Pieter a fool. But his father did not.

"Pieter is a dreamer," he said. "He knows beyond things. He understands the songs of the birds. And if he prefers the company of dumb plants and animals to that of people, perhaps it is a wise choice. It is not for me to say."

But the people of the village felt it was for them to say. They said so many unkind things about Pieter that the miller grew sad. At last Pieter said to him, "Father, I will go and seek my fortune. Then, perhaps, both you and I will have peace from this ceaseless wagging of mischievous tongues."

And so Pieter made his way into the wide, wide world.

He had traveled only two days and three nights into the wide, wide world when he heard a weak cry. It sounded like a call for help. Immediately, and without a thought for his own safety, Pieter rushed in the direction of the sound and found a tiny brown bird caught in a trap. He opened the trap and set the bird free. But the bird was so weak from lack of water and food that it only had time for a few faint chirps before it folded its tired wings and died.

However, since Pieter could speak the language of the birds, those few chirps were enough to tell him something of great importance. He hurried off to a nearby tree, where a nest lay concealed in the topmost branches.

In the nest was a single egg, gleaming like marble, white and veined with red and gold. Pieter picked it up. He thought about what the dying bird had told him: "In the egg lives the bird of time. When the egg is broken open, the bird will emerge singing. As long as it continues to sing, time will flow onward like a river. But if you should hold the bird and say, '*Bird of time, make time go fast,*' time will speed up for everyone except yourself and those you hold until you loose the bird again. And," the dying bird had continued, "if you say, '*Bird of time, make time go slow,*' time will slow down for everyone around. And you and those you hold will run through time like the wind through leafless trees."

Then the little brown bird had shivered all over. "But never say, '*Bird of time, make time stop,*' for then there will be a great shaking and a great quaking and time will stop for you and those you hold for evermore."

With that, the bird had cried out, "Good friend, good-by," and died.

Pieter was awed by this but not overawed, for he was a dreamer

and dreamers believe in miracles, both large and small. So he put the egg in his cap, his cap on his head, and journeyed farther into the wide, wide world.

He had hardly been gone another night and day when suddenly there came a second cry for help. This time it was not a little cry, but a great weeping and a wailing and a terrible sobbing that filled the entire kingdom through which he was traveling.

Once again, without a thought for his own safety, Pieter ran toward the sound. Soon he came upon a large palace. Before it was a crowd of men and women and children. They were all crying and moaning, twisting their kerchiefs or stomping on their caps.

"What is the matter?" asked Pieter. "Is there something wrong?"

"You must be worse than a fool," said an old man. "For even a fool could see that we weep and cry because the wicked giant has just now stolen the king's daughter dear and carried her off to Castle Gloam. And none of us is brave enough or smart enough or strong enough to rescue her."

"Well, then, I must," said Pieter.

"Indeed you *are* a fool," said another man. "For if we, who are the people of the mightiest king in the world, are not brave enough or smart enough or strong enough to rescue the princess, then only a fool would try."

"Fool I may be," said Pieter, "or worse. But I think you are more foolish than I if you will not try at all."

And off he went with not a word more toward Castle Gloam to rescue the king's beautiful daughter.

Pieter walked and walked seven days and seven nights to Castle Gloam, which teetered on the edge of the world (for in those days the world was flat). At last he found the castle and pushed through the enormous door.

It was nearly dark inside the castle, and cold. A single light shone dimly at the end of a long hall. It was toward that light that Pieter walked. When he came to where the light began and the hall ended, he saw the king's daughter. She was sitting on a golden throne in a golden cage and weeping as though her tears could wash away the bars.

"Do not cry," said Pieter when he was quite close to the cage. "I am here to bring you home." He spoke bravely, although he had no idea how to accomplish what he promised.

When she heard him, the king's daughter looked up, her eyes

shimmering with tears. And when she looked at him, Pieter felt her gaze go straight to his heart; he had never seen anyone so beautiful. He knelt before her and took off his cap. And the egg, which had been hidden there, nestled in his hair.

Just then he heard loud footsteps and a giant voice shouting.

And before Pieter could move, the floors shook and the walls trembled and the giant of Castle Gloam stomped into the room.

Pieter turned around to stare at the giant. And as he turned, the egg, which had been nestled in his hair, fell off his head and broke

upon the floor. A little brown bird arose singing from the broken egg and alighted on Pieter's hand.

Pieter stood up. Reaching into the cage, he took the hand of the king's daughter gently in his. Then he said, *"Bird of time, make time go slow."*

Immediately the little brown bird began singing a very slow, measured song. And time, which had been flowing along like a swift river, suddenly became muddy and slow for the giant. And he moved awkwardly through the air as though it were water.

Without letting go of the princess's hand, Pieter quickly opened the cage with a golden key he found hanging nearby. The king's

daughter ran out. Then hand in hand they raced out into the countryside like the wind through leafless trees. There they danced and laughed. And Pieter threw his arms up into the air with joy, and the bird of time was loosed.

At once time began to move normally again. In a moment Pieter and the princess heard the loud, rattling footsteps of the giant as he searched through Castle Gloam for the king's daughter.

"Quickly," said Pieter, taking the princess by the hand. "We must run."

But run as fast as they could, they could not run faster than the giant. With loud, earth-shattering footsteps, he gained at every stride.

"Save yourself!" cried the king's daughter. "It is foolish to stay with me."

But Pieter merely held out his hand, and the bird of time flew down and nestled in it.

"Lie down," said Pieter to the king's daughter. And he lay down by her side in the tall meadow grass.

"Bird of time, make time go fast," commanded Pieter.

The little brown bird began to sing a light, quick song. And time sped up for everyone but Pieter and the lovely princess.

The giant fairly flew over to the two bodies lying side by side on the ground. He twirled around and about them. To his speeded-up eyes they seemed dead, so measured and slow was their breathing. The giant gnashed his teeth in rage at having lost his beautiful captive. Hastily he pounded his fists on the ground. Then he noticed the bird of time in Pieter's hand singing a light, quick song. Forgetting the princess, he tore the bird out of Pieter's hand with a swift, sharp, angry movement.

Gloating, the giant ran back to Castle Gloam with the bird. Pieter and the princess watched him go.

Now the giant had heard what Pieter had said to the bird, and he realized that there was magic about. He thought that if the bird could make time speed up or make time slow down, it could help him conquer the world. And because he was evil and exceptionally greedy, the giant thought what a great fortune he could gather and how many beautiful princesses he could steal, if time could be stopped altogether and no one but he could move at all.

He put out his hand as he had seen Pieter do, and the bird nestled into it, almost disappearing in his vast palm.

"Bird of time," he commanded, *"make time stop!"*

And the bird of time stopped singing.

The giant did not know that this was a calamitous thing to say. He had not heard the dying bird's warning that no one can make time stop altogether. And he was too wicked to worry about it on his own.

Suddenly there was a great quaking. And a great shaking. The rocks that Castle Gloam stood upon began to crack. Fissures appeared in the walls. The roof began to tremble. Then, very slowly, Castle Gloam slid over the edge of the world and disappeared.

And inside the lost castle the giant and the silent bird of time were caught forever in a timeless scream.

Pieter and the king's daughter watched as the castle sank out of

sight. As soon as the castle disappeared over the edge of the world, the world returned to normal again. Once more time flowed onward like a river.

Then Pieter and the princess looked at one another and smiled. And hand in hand they walked back for seven days and seven nights until they reached the palace of the king.

There Pieter and the princess were married amidst great singing and dancing. In due time, Pieter himself became king, and lived a long and full life with his beautiful wife always at his side.

And though Pieter had found another egg veined with red and gold nestled in his cap right after the bird and the giant had disappeared, he was never fool enough to tell. Instead he gave the egg into the keeping of his father, Honest Hans. And the old miller buried it under the mill in a wooden box, where it has remained safe and unbroken to this very day.

ABOUT THE AUTHOR

JANE YOLEN is a versatile writer of many distinguished books for young people. Her informational book about kites, *World on a String,* was chosen as an A.L.A. Notable Book, and her humorous novels are beloved by children, but her finest writing has been reserved for her picture-stories, a growing group of beautiful books including the award-winning *Emperor and the Kite.*

Jane Yolen, born in New York, was graduated from Smith College. She now lives with her husband and their three small children in a lovely old house not far from Boston. She worked for a time as an editor of children's books with a large New York publisher before deciding to devote herself to writing. She is also an accomplished folk-singer, often accompanying herself on the guitar, autoharp, and fairy bells.

ABOUT THE ILLUSTRATOR

MERCER MAYER has in a short time risen to the top echelon of illustrators of books for children. His first book, *A Boy, a Dog, and a Frog,* published in 1967, was a delightful story told entirely in eloquent pictures without any words. Since then his imaginative and technically accomplished illustrations have been seen in a growing list of books, and in 1970 he was chosen to create the poster for National Children's Book Week. His illustrations for *The Bird of Time,* exquisitely executed in tempera, evoke the earthy charm of the peasant life of sixteenth-century Flanders, recalling the scenes that Breughel and Teniers loved to paint.

Mercer Mayer and his wife Marianna, who is also an artist, like to collaborate on books. Mr. Mayer's paintings are exhibited at Gallery Madison 90 in New York City. The Mayers now live in Sea Cliff, New York.